A Special Baby

Written By:
IRENE KOTTER

Illustrations Provided By:
Welsh Holdings

Idea Creations Press
www.ideacreationpress.com

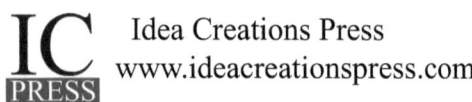

Idea Creations Press
www.ideacreationspress.com

978-1-948804-07-3

Publisher's Catalog-In-Publishing Data

Kotter, Irene, author
Welsh Holdings, illustrations
A Special Baby
First trade paperback original edition | Salt Lake City: Idea Creations Press, 2018.
ISBN 978-1-948804-07-3 |LCCN 2018962850
Designed by Douglas L. Jones
Children's Picture Book, Children's Christian, Jesus | BIASC: JUVENILE NONFICTION / Religion / Bible Stories / New Testament

Printed in the U.S.A.

A huge thank you to my family and friends, to Sherri at Costume Castle in Layton, Utah, for her help with the outfits for the pictures, and a huge hug to those who posed for me or allowed their children to do the same. I appreciate you!

"Come here, son,"
his mother called.

"What is it, Momma?"
the son asked
as he walked to her.

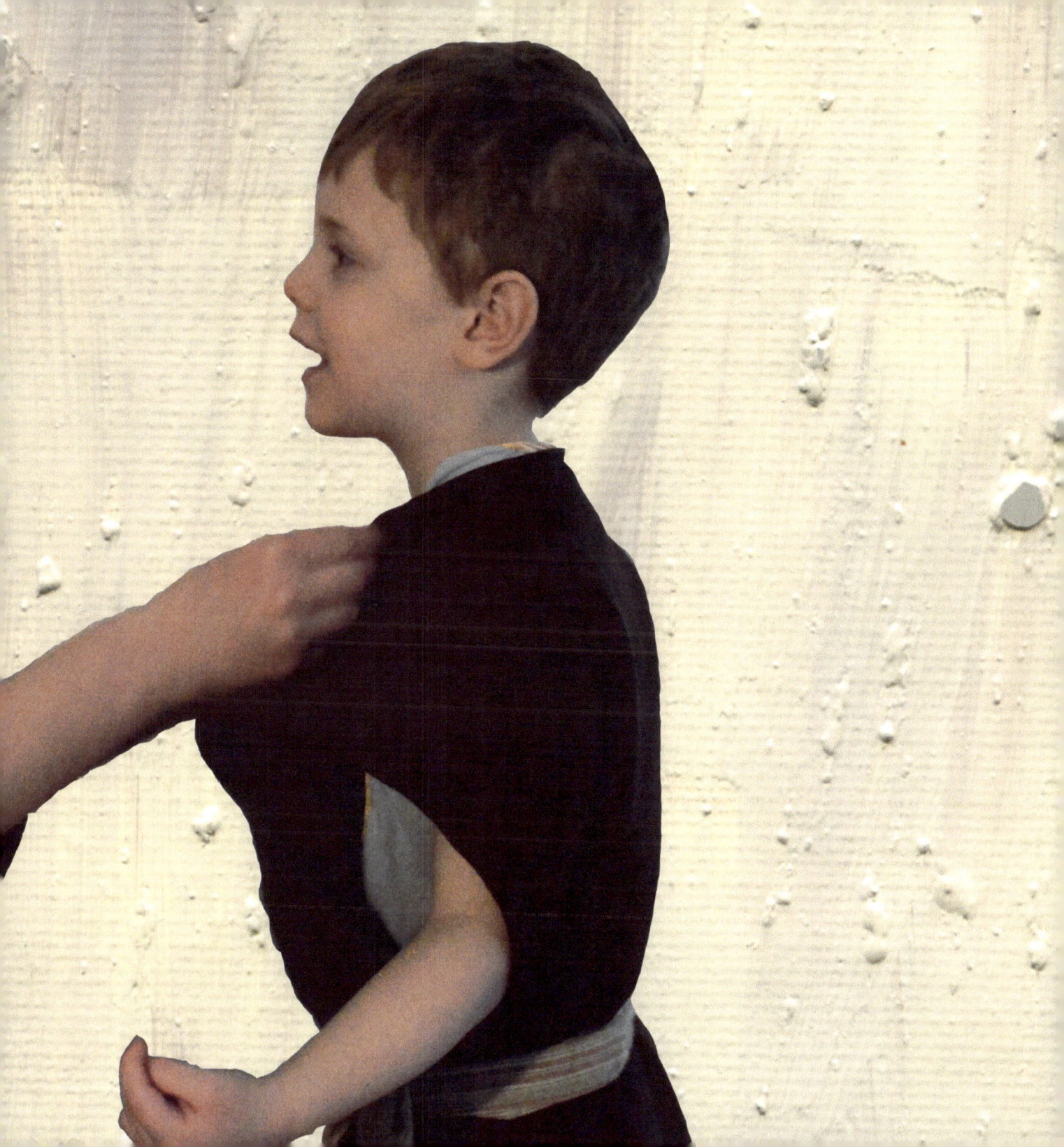

"It's about a young woman and a man who were blessed by God with a baby, a very special baby!" she answered.

"There was a young woman.
She did her best
to follow the Lord's
commandments.
She was not married,
but was engaged to a good man.
One day, she met a stranger,
who was an angel of the Lord.
He told her great things,
one of which was that
she would soon be a mother
to a very special child.
She was honored
to be his mother."

"Why was the baby special?" the boy asked.

"He is the Son of God, destined to do great and marvelous things. He is a blessing from above to bless the lives of all he meets," she answered.

"Now, there was a righteous man who lived not far away. He was preparing for his wedding to that young woman. While he was thinking about his wedding, he fell asleep, and had a special dream. An angel of the Lord told him about how the baby was to be the Son of God. He was also told to marry the young woman."

"A short time later, they were married."

"Yes, my son.
YOU are that special baby.
You are God's child! He loves
you and has blessed me to be
your mother. He has given
me the great responsibility of
helping you know
who you really are."

"You have many great resposibilities in your future. You are God's child. It will not always be easy to make the right choices, and there will be times you will struggle. However, if you will remember who you are, you will have the strength to succeed."

"What do you mean?"

"You are God's child, and no
matter what happens, He is
there. You can talk to Him,
even though you cannot see
him. You can feel Him when
your heart is full and it feels
like a blanket has been placed
around you. That is God saying
He is there and He is listening.

"I have that feeling now, Momma," Jesus said, softly.

"That is His way of telling you what I am saying is true," she answered reverently.

"How can I know what the right choice is?" He asked.

"He can talk to you, too. The thoughts and feelings that come into your heart and mind along with that feeling of the safe warm blanket, that is when He is talking to you."

"I love you,
and so does God. He is
your father! Always
remember who you are,
no matter what anyone
else may say. Remember
you are His child and
He loves you!"

"I will, Momma. I will."

www.ingramcontent.com/pod-product-compliance
Lightning Source LLC
Chambersburg PA
CBHW041620120626
46551CB00003B/523